Born of Water

A Hybrid Novelette

Constance Malloy

Karen –
May your waters be
calm.

Best –
Connie Malloy

ELJ Editions, Ltd. is committed to publishing works of quality and integrity. In that spirit, we are proud to offer this novelette collection to our readers. This novelette is a work of fiction. Names, characters, places, and incidents either are the product of the author's imagination or are used fictitiously, and any resemblance to actual persons, living or dead, business establishments, events, or locales is entirely coincidental.

ISBN: 978-1-941617-73-1

Cover Design by ELJ Editions, Ltd.
Illustrated by Hannah Malloy

ELJ Publications (Imprint)
ELJ Editions, Ltd.
P.O. Box 815
Washingtonville, NY 10992

www.elj-editions.com

Praise for Born of Water

Born of Water, by Constance Malloy, is like nothing I've ever read before—part fairy tale, part meta, part speculative, part grounded in reality, it addresses family dynamics, especially maternal relationships, but also Mother Earth and climate change through the fabulous character Mari and her obituaries of dead lakes. Ultimately, this is a story of the need to do things differently, both on a personal and global level, to learn from our mistakes. The writing is assured, sometimes poetic, sometimes provocative, and always engaging. I defy anyone to do anything other than read this story in one sitting. I know I will read it again and again and find more to love each time. A stunning achievement. —Karen Jones, author of *Burn It All Down*

Born of Water is a deep exploration of opposites: nature as both salvation and ruin, humanity's tiny and outsized footprint, and family as a structure both to be protected and protected from. In a smooth allegory that bleeds into realism through the invention of character, where Mari demands the writer's ear, Malloy also deeply draws the reader into the world. —Al Kratz, author of *Off the Resting Sea*

Subversive in structure and narrative, *Born of Water* is awash with heartbreak and healing, disaster and devotion, tragedy and triumph. Rippling with beautiful imagery and stunning creativity, Malloy's writing sweeps you on a journey that plumbs the depths of emotion, questions the ties that bind, and cumulates in a watershed of revelatory wonder. Part psychodrama, part eco-fiction, and wholly original, *Born of Water* begs to be read again as soon as it's finished. —Audra Kerr Brown, author of *hush hush hush*

Allegorical but personal, vision-laden then soberly real, *Born of Water* is like nothing I've ever read before. It bridges familial trauma and ecological devastation, marries mysticism with materiality, and mines dreams and disasters. A lesser talent might have made a muddle of such disparate threads, but Constance Malloy is a deft weaver, and she nets us utterly. The paradox of this mercurial hybrid is the pure distillation its complexities effect, a winnowing to essence, to the most integral, elemental us. "We stared in disbelief at the splendor of it all," Malloy writes. "This was, as my grandfather would say, powerful medicine." I love the beautiful philosophy these words suggest. *Born of Water* reminds us the world is saturated with mystery—or "splendor" or "powerful medicine." We have only to see it. —Melissa Ostrom, author of *The Beloved Wild* and *Unleaving*

Author Constance Malloy blends fantasy and reality, fiction and non-fiction in an utterly original story of escaping a dysfunctional family. You will fall in love with Mari, the story-within-the story character who writes obituaries for bodies of water dying due to climate change. In parallel with the stunning creatures of air and ocean featured in this novelette, we are taken on a ride of highs and lows, the grace of love and the horrors of verbal abuse. Riveted from start to finish, I can honestly say I've never read anything like *Born of Water*. Malloy is a hugely talented writer. —Lisa Alletson, author of *Good Mother Lizard*

For my soul sister,
Kris Roberts

Contents

Part One

    I.   Hawk's Breath   3
    II.   Heron's Flight   18

Part Two

Ebb

    I.   A Moment from 2021 in the Present Tense   26
    II.   Fresh (Water) Start   28
    III. Four Months Later   37
    IV. The Source   45

Flow

PART ONE

I

Hawk's Breath

1

It's problematic raising a child on a cliff. Especially when continual upward movement is required. It is a destressing yet necessary lesson to teach your child, whether on a cliff or on the ground, that one wrong move in life will kill you. As a result, our daughter learned never to look down and not to press up until her footing was certain.

"How do I know when it's certain?" Grace asked, along with all the "whys" and "how comes" a child needs the answers to time and time again.

"Here," my husband patiently directed. "Put your foot on my knee."

Each time he steadied his knee against her weight, he'd ask, "How does it feel?" The calm he forced upon his leg conveyed to our growing child that while her parents' foundation had crumbled beneath them, her foundation grew more stable and more predictable daily.

We are not cliff climbers by practice. There are no carabiners to secure ropes, no belay devices or belayers below. We are tethered to nothing but the ropes of familial dysfunction, anchoring us to the dynamics we are willfully, consciously, trying to break. Ropes pulled by desperate hands, fueled by an unrelenting desire to defend the status quo. Ropes attached telepathically to our minds, whispering their seductions of the familial familiar in our ears.

Not until after several grounded, sober attempts to explain to our husbandless mothers and our siblings why we did not want to raise our daughter within the dysfunctional dynamics our mothers had spawned from their need to protect their unconscious fears and secrets through factionalization, passive aggression, narcissism, and emotional abuse; not until after our mother's unrelenting protests and denials of the dynamics' existence and the power of generational drift; not until after our siblings, trapped within the fog of their entanglement and their co-conspirators' roles of enablers were rendered deaf to the language of codependency and trauma recovery, causing them to deny their alcoholism, eating disorders, and dysfunctional marriages as the proliferation of the dynamics; not until after our mothers and siblings admonished us with accusations of possessing uncaring, selfish hearts did we, finally, accept that in order to save our daughter from the inertia caused by the enclosed, myopic realities our families inhabited, we'd have to climb.

A climb that required a thousand feet for each of her now fourteen years.

In her infancy, we passed her small, swaddled self between us with little effort. I treasured the warmth of her cheek against my chest when it was my turn to support her weight. The scent of her peach-fuzzed head propelled me to place one hand, one foot, above the other and keep climbing. Never looking down, but only up; even when at the time, the cliff's ledge was so high, so out of sight, I wondered if the summit existed. Knowing that everything about her life depended upon us made the endeavor to place every step with determined intention more fraught.

Finding a crevice, large or small, to slip in a hand or a foot, or a shallow protrusion for grabbing or pressing was the only action of our monotonous, mission-filled days. Not unlike the universal monotony of parenting an infant: sleep, feed, diaper change, repeat. During her days of toddlerhood, we filled her head full of dinosaurs and horses, Greek mythology, and various religious stories. At night, when rest was so necessary but so dangerous, we lulled her to sleep, pointing out constellations and the Milky Way. Marveling at how dark the night sky was, we convinced her its black-velveted dome was the blanket of the universe protecting us from unseen nocturnal monsters. We sang songs like "It's only a Paper Moon," "Twinkle, Twinkle, Little Star," and "The Alphabet Song." We avoided singing about boughs breaking and cradles falling.

We filled the passing days, months, years, of her early childhood with the stories of *Star Trek*. We recounted the escapades of Kirk and Spock, the adventures of Picard and *The Next Generation*, and Sisko's joining of the Celestial Temple in *DS9*. These tales seemed an effective way to instill in Grace the belief that a different, better future was worth the fight.

From the dawn of each waxing morning until the gloam of each waning day, we persisted upward, methodically increasing Grace's responsibility for her own climb until we became six hands reaching up and six feet pressing on.

As we became more successful in our climb, and Grace entered her pre-teen years, the inability of our mothers to convert her began to vex them with the utmost vexing, fueling a witchery in them we could not, did not, predict.

Our now desperate witch-mothers attacked us on multiple fronts, conjuring minions in myriad forms, but none as threatening as the you-owe-me mites.

Such an invasive species, the you-owe-me mites. These are special mites with queens like bees or ants. These queens, in a constant state of rapid birth, fire out eggs maturing from larvae to nymph to adult within two days.

Sent up the cliff by the deprived grandmothers, the you-owe-me mites approached like an army of pinhead-sized Trojans. The multitude of their tiny legs clicking against the rock echoed throughout the canyon. Their nipping, biting mouths attacked in a chorus of you-owe-mes:

You owe me absolute fealty.

You owe me absolution from the accountability of my actions.

You owe me self-abandonment through becoming my friend, my therapist, my confessor, my spouse.

You owe me the ability to manipulate your young as I have manipulated you.

You Owe Me!

As the you-owe-me mites grew battle weary, our siblings sent in reinforcements, the you-owe-her mites. These mites bit harder. Demanded more blood. But when it dawned on these you-owe-her mites, who had so obediently followed the orders of the you-owe-me mites, that we were refusing to participate in what they perceived to be our shared, biologically induced, duties and obligations, they got mad. Real mad.

"Who do you think you are?" they shouted.

We tried to reason with them, stating the you-owe-me mites were asking things that weren't fair of anyone to ask. We argued, "Biology doesn't grant the right to abuse."

We stated repeatedly, while probing for hand holds and foot holds and shielding Grace from their incessant biting, that our actions weren't about not loving them or our mothers but were about not wanting to live inside the dynamics our mothers had created, where unquestioned loyalty, no matter the personal costs to their children or grandchildren, was demanded.

"We love Grace too much to condemn her to this future," we said.

"Why are you hurting us like this? Don't you love us?" The you-owe-her mites pleaded, having collectively misconstrued our act of self-preservation as one of defiance and abandonment.

"Join us," we shouted down the cliff. "It doesn't have to be this way."

But the you-owe-her mites continued to wage war, and we continued to climb. All the while, our mother-witches stood, smiling an odd, victorious, sideways smile, knowing no matter how much their other children might imagine, even desire, to climb into something different, theirs' would be a short-lived escape. Our siblings were simply unable to eradicate their own you-owe-me mite infestations.

We encouraged our mothers to join us too, but they had slept with their fears under frayed blankets, thinned with age like skin and hair, for decades. This, in their minds, was far safer than waking to a world where their truths were uncovered.

As the enabler mites weakened and began to withdraw, our siblings lifted their faces towards us, displaying a collective countenance warped by a lack of understanding of their wanting. In the distance, we heard our mothers, their voices bold, ricocheting throughout the canyon, coaching our siblings' perceptions. "You," they directed, "stayed because you love me."

Several hundred feet above the mites' retreat, we emerged above the tree line. Of course, trees are sparse on sheer cliff faces, but still, we had long passed the mountain's capability of supporting habitat. It was at this point our mothers rallied their last offensive strike and sent a flock of gulls, calling out a collective ha-ha-ha, up the cliffside.

Their attack forced us into yet another war of attrition. This one, lasting nearly two years, ended with them squawking their disapproval at our sore, tired backs, pocked by their relentless jabs. Sweat and blood trickled in equal proportions downward, pooling in the small curve of our lower spines. The gulls finally ceased when our sustained defense exhausted their fight.

Perhaps the unanticipated convocation of eagles circling above the cliff's ledge scared them away. Our tenacity? The convocation? We didn't care which. After flapping their wings one last time at our heads, they flew away in search of less resilient prey.

Our journey, simply put, had been arduous; and admittedly, I felt my resiliency fading. Looking towards the circling eagles, their white heads brilliant in the reflected sunlight, I asked them to please keep rotating above. Every time one flew over the empty space, expanding downward into the fjord of our past, I saw only the ledge. With it in my sights, I could, I would, will myself to make it just that much further.

Our journey culminated on an early autumn day at sunrise. Pink-edged clouds drifted about the sky with an ease I longed for as my tension increased with each new placement of hand and foot. The sun warmed our bodies while slicking the cliff's chocolate surface with dew; the result of a frost-inducing night.

The eagles, now perched on the cliff ledge, stood like the sentinels of Easter Island. Racing against the ebb of my strength, I coerced my body upwards the last hundred feet of our ascent with my sights fixed on their yellow beaks and alert eyes.

Grace's adolescent muscles flexed as she maneuvered towards her protectors. As our event horizon neared, I saw in her a young person who had grown more confident in the placement of her own feet upon the knife's edge she had been raised. She no longer struggled against her yearning for the level ground beneath her feet that she imagined others had. I watched her maturity blossom as she embraced the painful realization that achieving one's goals often meant sacrificing one's wants. With youth on her side, and a desire for this journey to end, she sprinted the last several yards to the ledge where the eagles' awe-inspiring talons gripped the rim.

My fingers, raw and tired, cramped as I reached the summit. "Please," I asked my husband, "can we rest for a moment?"

A brief panic coursed through his countenance. Afraid, I presumed, that if I stopped, I would lose my momentum, allowing fatigue to settle, not only in me, but in him and Grace as well, arresting us so close to the end.

The sun disappeared behind towering white clouds, allowing a cool breeze to comfort my spent body. "I'll be able to make it," I said, hoping to assuage his fear. "It's just that," I paused. In that moment of mental relaxation, the reality of our climb registered inside me and demanded I acknowledge the truth of the sacrifice required to reach our endgame. The victory of self-preservation, I had to own, brought with it a weightier price tag than I had wagered.

The price tag: we had to say goodbye to our families and grant them their preferred narratives of our actions. Those being: we had abandoned them; we didn't love them; we were shirking our familial responsibilities. A cost, a loss, so great, I had to grieve it before continuing.

And so, for the first time since our climb commenced, I looked down.

Fourteen thousand feet is a dizzying height. Overcome with nausea, my stomach now fighting for an exit through my throat, I pressed my body closer to the cliff, as if that were even possible. A river, as wide as the Mississippi, cutting through the canyon below, looked no more than the thinnest pencil line etched upon the ground. I fancied it a Nazca Line offering me an ancient, perhaps alien, message. I laughed with sadness and understanding.

I pulled my gaze back to Grace, "Remember," I implored with tears welling in my eyes. "They love you very much. And your father and I love them very much too."

My husband concurred and paid reverence to what he was leaving behind as well.

"I know," she said. "I won't forget them. I'll miss them too. But you're right," she exhaled, looking into the abyss. "I don't want to live down there."

Dizzy, she faltered and leaned into her father. Her discomfort was a worthy ally. Visual proof of the vast distance she had traveled was a valuable truth to possess. To rob her of this knowledge, no matter how uncomfortable it made her, would have denied her the rewards of successfully overcoming the struggles we had forced upon her.

Once our shared vertigo passed, we resumed our climb.

The eagles flew off the ledge and circled the wide expanse behind us. Protecting us, I believed, from any last attempts our mothers might make to thwart us. My husband and I reached one hand up, digging our bleeding fingers into dirt and rock. Securing our hold, we supported our daughter with our free hands as she scaled the rim. With immense effort, she hoisted herself over the top. She quickly turned and peered down at us.

"Grace," my husband ordered, "get as far back as possible. Don't worry about us. Just get yourself safely away from the ledge."

Panic gripped her, but she obeyed.

"I'll go first, so I can help you up," he said.

Visions of me slipping and pulling him over, the two of us headfirst, limbs akimbo, rushing downward away from our daughter, raced through my mind.

"No," I said. "We've made this journey together, and we'll summit together."

He smiled, understanding that was code for *the chances of at least one of us surviving are greater this way.*

With a herculean heave, I pressed up until my chest rested on the jagged, rocky lip.

"We've got this," he said, right as I felt talons clasp my shoulders. I watched two eagles, one at each arm, fly my husband to safety. Seeing my mirror, I surrendered my weight to our winged saviors.

A verdant plateau dotted in pink and blue and white flowers stretched out before us. Awed, we stumbled when released from the eagles' hold. The air's fragrance, so fresh, so not of stone and rock, awoke in me memories of gardens and water and life. The faint outline of rolling hills emerged from the horizon. Or were those clouds? The austerity of the scene evoked the sacred.

We regained our footing and agreed when our daughter said, "It's so peaceful here."

We stood, unable to move. We had arrived at a place unknown. Where were we to go? What were we to do?

"I think the most important thing right now," my husband's voice joined the buzzing of bees swarming the plateau floor, "is to put some distance between us and the ledge and then rest." Inhaling deep and long, he exhaled and added, "It's been a long climb."

Grace and I chuckled. Framing what we had just endured as a long climb would forever live in our collective annals of the colossally understated.

But within a few steps, the ropes anchoring us to our mothers once again pulled taut. Odd how something invisible had unmistakable mass and tension and intention. Refusing defeat, we walked in a shared posture, chest lifted, pressed forward in the ankles, pulling against, not bracing from, the voracious neediness of our mothers. A neediness proven to exist in a cavern so deep, it lacked any ability to be sated.

As we forged on, the ropes, unknown to us, were fraying against the cliff's serrated edge. When the last thread gave way, all tension gone in mid-step, we reeled head over foot for several yards.

Grace chased after us calling, "Mom! Dad! Are you okay?"

We came to rest, flat on our backs, looking up into the now, cloudless sky. Grace, on her knees between us, trembled and cried, even as we reassured her, we were physically unharmed. We granted her the necessary time to release all she had held in during these fourteen years. Not until night, did her body calm.

All splayed onto the plateau's surface, the cool of the soporific grass comforting our somnolent bodies, we succumbed.

"Mom," Grace said. Her voice slurry in near sleep. "What if the bad birds come back?"

Rubbing her arm, I offered reassurance, "I will make sure they don't."

As I closed my eyes, the shadow of a winged creature passed in front of the moon, now at its apex. I felt the rush of air when the predator landed beside my skyward face. Brushing my temple with the crown of his feather-soft head, his breath warm upon my cheek, he asked, "Do you remember me?"

I did not need to look to know who had come to offer safety.

"Of course, I do," I said. A calm only the deepest trust can conjure washed over me. "I've never forgotten you. How could I?"

2

Grace was preceded in this life by two miscarriages and a blighted ovum pregnancy. The first of those miscarriages expired the week before Thanksgiving in 2003. Upon becoming pregnant, J and I had not conceived of the potentiality of a miscarriage. The day I returned from the ultrasound, confirming our combined creation no longer thrived within my womb, we cried together, cleaved upon the foyer floor where J had collapsed when I shared the news.

The Sunday night before Thanksgiving (four days after my D&C), a bird became trapped in our fireplace flue. Fatigued by momentum abruptly halted a few days before, we turned the light out and delayed dealing with the creature until morning. But on Monday and Tuesday, in the absence of any rustling or brushing of feathers against the metal liner of the flue womb, it seemed apparent the bird, like our child, had expired.

On Wednesday afternoon, as I passed the fireplace to gaze out our front windows, a flurry of wing brushing metal startled me. The creature had been alive; and we, projecting our loss upon this helpless being, had counted him/her/it dead.

I phoned J at work. Wracked with guilt that we had added to the bird's suffering, and not knowing anything about how to free one trapped within, we agreed I should research best practices before attempting its rescue. A Google search proved my intuition correct. The bird required daylight to escape. As it was already dusk, on a cloudy afternoon, we prayed the bird would survive the night. We planned to free it in the morning before joining J's family for Thanksgiving.

After an early breakfast, we covered the living room windows except a long, narrow one furthest from the fireplace. We removed the screen and fully opened the window. We lived in an upper flat, and since the cloud cover had persisted, I hoped it might help that we were closer to the sky than the ground. I left the room as J rested a flashlight, pointed upward, on the iron grate. He turned on the light and tiptoed out of the room. He joined me behind the swinging door, separating the living room from the foyer.

We peered through the slightest crack. Our gazes locked on the fireplace. We waited. Our stomachs, tight. Our breaths, shallow. What would emerge?

"Do you think it's a cardinal?" I whispered.

"It's probably one of those pesky house…" before he finished, astonishment arrested our breath when a large head with a predator's beak peeked out from the under the flue.

He looked to the right and then to the left. He paused. Stunned, we watched as he lowered the hulk of his body and perched upon the grate. The three of us remained motionless until he began surveying the room, swiveling his head from us to the window.

There was a hawk in our living room! Perched on our fireplace grate! Who had been stuck in our flue for at least five days! How could that be? Especially since the chimney top had recently been repaired. New screens and all. How did a hawk get into the fireplace?

We stared in disbelief at the splendor of it all. This was, as my grandfather would say, powerful medicine.

Then we, along with every creature within a small radius of our flat, were silenced when the hawk bore down and with one flap extended his wings upon take off. With his aviator's precision, he rotated 180 degrees and exited through the window. The tips of his fully spanned wings nearly touched the top and bottom of the sill. The red tail feathers that gave him his name barely missed the frame.

We exhaled and rushed to the window.

"Look," J said, as we watched the hawk soar over the leafless treetops to the west. "He's flying to the river for water."

3

We awoke on an early autumn day at sunrise. Refreshed, I sat and absorbed warmth from the orange-fired orb barely cresting the purple-hued hills. Pink-edged clouds flitted about the sky as the sun's ever-lengthening rays transformed the dew-dappled flowers and grasses of the plateau into a glistening meadow bespeckled in a multitude of crystals.

Eyes closed, I inhaled the moist morning air. I felt a nudge upon my leg and looked to find the hawk, my guardian, tall at my side. Unafraid, I ran my hand down his white-feathered, brawny chest, kissed the top of his head, and said thank you.

I lowered my head until we were beak to nose. In his long, articulate exhalation, I heard, Na-Ha-Li. And so, I named him.

With a flying hop, Nahali approached Grace first and then J. He caressed their legs with his beak. Was he kissing them?

We stood, stretched, and wondered how long we had slept.

"I'm thirsty," Grace said.

Nahali answered with a descending *kee-aah* and took to the sky. Circling over our heads, he screeched, *kee-aah. Follow me. Kee-aah. Follow me.*

And so we did; westward, into a steaming fog lifting from the warming ground.

As the fog retreated, we were no longer on the plateau but walking the familiar terrain near our home on a Sunday afternoon. We passed the gnarled, lightning-singed trunk of the weeping willow. We entered, as ritual demanded, the wigwam made from naturally felled birch trees.

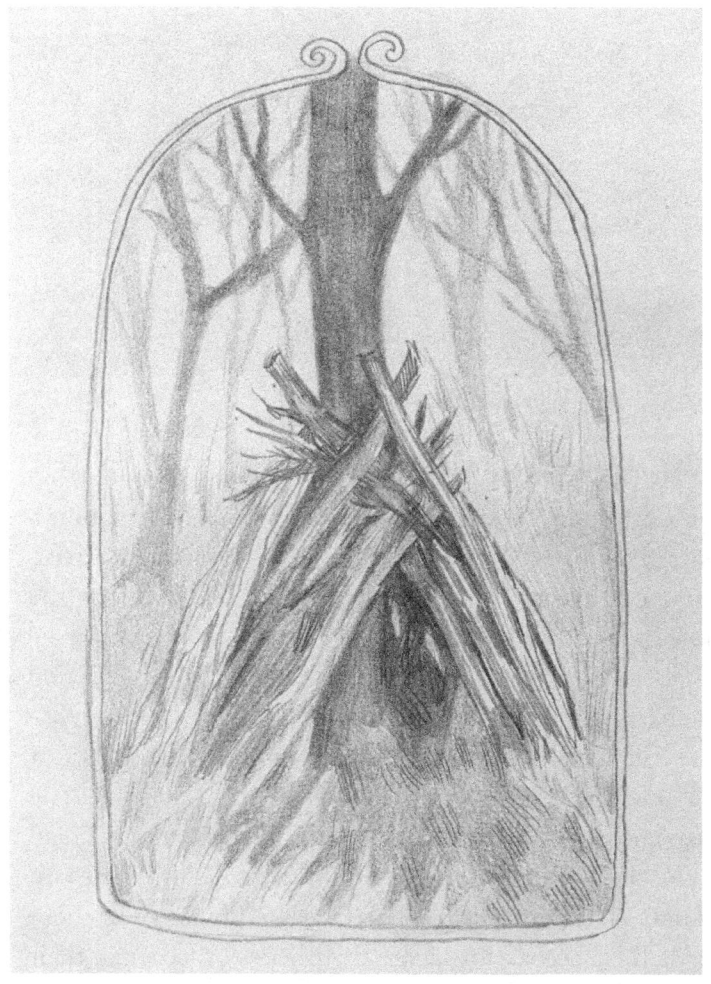

"Look," Grace said, pointing to the sky as we walked upon reeds laid flat from receding flood waters. "Nahali's followed us to the river."

II

Heron's Flight

1

Nahali, screeching his presence in the sky, accompanies me on my daily meditative visits to the river. Our bond, unbreakable. We are paired savior/survivor, survivor/savior from a time before our knowing into the time beyond our knowing.

At the wigwam, Nahali signals his departure, leaving me to my thoughts.

Lately, I have been consumed by the many bodies of water evaporating worldwide. The Great Salt Lake. The Dead (dying) Sea. Lake Como. Lake Mead. Recently, I read about the Uros who live on the shrinking Lake Titicaca on islands made of totora reeds. They also build from these reeds their homes for living, their beds for sleeping, their community huts for gathering, their boats for fishing, their baskets for selling to tourists who disembark during lake cruises to visit their island homes. This seems to me a most efficient use of one's resources. But as Lake Titicaca loses volume, the totora reeds are no longer substantial enough to make their islands, their homes, their beds, their huts, their boats, their baskets.

I imagine the Uros living a life of eternal womb comfort. Their island reed beds gently brushed side to side by the water's current. What, I wonder, would it be like to always be upon the water? What, I wonder more, would it be like to have the actions/greed/foolishness of a people you've never met, from a place you've never been, force you to abandon the water life of your ancestors that dates back many centuries before the founding of the resource-guzzling U S of A?

I approach the Menomonee River and stop at a favorite spot along its banks where an elongated S-curve rushes the water to the south. I listen to the gush over stone and the red-wing blackbird's conk-la-ree. I see the froth of small waves and a dragonfly hover above the shallows. A rustling in the brush pulls my attention across the bed. With ears pricked, a honey-brown doe watches me cautiously.

This river is a half mile west of my home. Lake Michigan is six miles due east. I cannot imagine being without water. I can't imagine living landlocked. I can't imagine watching my water source, my home, disappear in my lifetime. I can't imagine the mindset that puts capitalism before humanism. So much, I can't imagine. And yet, so much I can.

2

On a languid morning, I walk the banks of the Menomonee River and delight in the force of its raging current. Swollen from the two inches of rain we received overnight, the river rushes from its past into its future, reminding me that the present is nothing more than a liminal blip between the two. My thoughts, as they so often do these days, center on the collective dilemma we all face with climate change. Some places are fighting erasure from rising oceans like Nyangai Island, Sierra Leone, and Venice; some places are scorched and parched like India and the American Southwest; some places have burned like Canada, Greece, and Hawaii; and our earth place, on any given day, is devastated by it all. Our individual climate change experience is irrevocably linked to our GPS location. Our collective experience, irrevocably linked by gravity, keeps us bound to and responsible for our shared, singular pale blue dot.

The seed of a new character sprouts from my ponderings of Lake Mead's dried, cracked waterbed. She has traveled inside my writer's womb for months, this woman born from my fascination with water and the extreme lack thereof. Conceived as a writer of obituaries for dying bodies of water, I have shared the idea of her with trusted friends (not yet wanting to place her too concretely on this plane for fear of a stillbirth), who liked her even before her naming.

Thinking of her, I pause, stunned by the beauty of a Great Blue Heron perched tall on a felled birch stretching across the riverbed. Her neck, relaxed and curved. A mallard family glides across the muddied water and disappears behind a peanut-shaped island between the heron and me. She doesn't move. I can tell from where I am she is an adult: her bulk and length, impressive. Nothing here knows of climate change. Nothing here has to care. At least not yet. The heron stretches long. She flutters her wings. She pulls the whole of her in and down, and then…everything stops as she releases the birch, and with one mighty flap, stretches her wings and soars past me, commanding the attention of all the river's inhabitants.

As I watch the heron follow the bend and fly down the river's center, I feel a tap upon the shoulder of my consciousness.

"I'm ready," I hear a voice say.

I turn to find her standing tall and lean like the heron. Her long, blue-black hair, catching in the breeze, lets me know she is ready to take flight from my imagination to the page.

"I am Mari," she names herself.

Mari. Hmm? Remove the i, and you have Mar. In English: to disfigure or to impair the appearance of a thing/person. In Spanish: sea. *Perhaps*, I think, *she will be transformed by the sea.*

Her presence demands my ear, so I find a smooth boulder along the river's edge and sit. The morning sun copper-tints my skin.

Believing a character's relationship with the author is an intimate dance predicated on the need for independence, which is necessitated by the need for dependence and borrowed experience, I promise Mari to listen to her story without interfering, and to open myself freely, so that she may take from me whatever is required for its telling.

PART TWO

Ebb

There was a girl born of water. In her youth, she ebbed and flowed with ease and grace, never questioning the moon's push and pull of her emotional tides. In the summer months, she swam in the waters of Lake Wapello, where, on some days, she fancied herself a dolphin. One of many in her pod. Fast and free, her fins cut the water as her flukes propelled her into a full body breach. Her rostrum high, inhaling the sun-heated air. With gleeful whistles, she arced wide and spun before returning to the surface. On other days, she assumed a narwhal, unicorn of the sea. On these days, she slowed and found pleasure exploring the depths of Artic waters with the other magical, elusive creatures in her blessing.

Her dolphin breaches with her pod and her narwhal explorations with her blessing allowed her to embed joy and comfort into her family's visits to Lake Wapello. But with each passing year, the visits began to expose her father's rage-filled irritations (whether he was with them or not), her mother's denial, and her older sister's withdrawal.

With her lungs made strong from swimming, she could capture copious amounts of oxygen, which she held at length before a sustained exhalation. This control created an illusion of coping for the girl born of water. It calmed her heightening fears and staved off the panic attacks she swallowed along with the truths she inhaled.

Years later, when her father called her at college to tell her he was leaving her mother, and added he was tired of the "obligations of parenthood" and the burden placed upon him by "your mother and you girls;" when he said, "I want more from life than this," and sounded all puffed up because he was "finally getting what I want, what I deserve;" and when he had the audacity to say to her, as she sat outside the campus library on an autumn day with red, orange, and yellow leaves raining all around her, two days before actually leaving her mother, "There's a friend of mine I'd really like you to meet. I think you'd like her a lot;" and then, when coming back from class three days later, she found her mother curled up in the fetal position on her bed announcing, "I'll never get over what your father has done to us," and how her crying smacked of play acting, of affecting the victim, and how her eyes searched for a reaction from the girl born of water, it was at that moment, she exchanged her rostrum and tusk for the long beak of the heron, her fins for the heron's wings, and moved out of the depths where she had raced and leapt and explored with her pod and her blessing into the shallows where she, in isolation, searched for her sustenance.

I

A Moment from 2021 in the Present Tense

Mari, twenty-two, is driving. Her mom is in the front seat. Her sister is in the back seat. It has been eleven years since Mari last traveled the rolling Iowa hills to Lake Wapello. It is early June, and the corn is low, undulating like a green ocean over the landscape.

"I can't believe I never knew this was a manmade lake," Mari says. As they ascend the last hill on their journey, she asks, "Why was it drained?"

"I don't think I want to know," her sister says.

"It had something to do with an invasive species. I think it's called gizzard shad," her mom says. "But they needed to repair the dam, too."

"How did they do it?" her sister rhetorically asks. "Is it like a tub with a big drain, and they just pulled the plug?"

Their laughing gives way to gasping as they summit the hill.

Even though Mari knew the lake had been drained, her brain had still anticipated the expanse of water, reflecting the sky and the surrounding woods, to stretch out before her upon cresting, but the gaping hole, filled with single-stocked reeds erupting out of its sandy bottom, startles her.

Without looking in the rearview mirror, she slams on the brakes. There, on top of the hill, with the parking lot, snack shack, and now endless beach below, something tugs in her. Something tells her she's safe here. Something tells her she's home.

She inches the car down the path to the parking lot and stops, facing the beach.

"Let's get out," Mari says.

"No way," her sister shouts. "What if the water suddenly comes rushing back?"

"You're crazy," Mari jeers. "Come on, Mom."

They walk to what they perceive to be the beach's edge, "Let's stay here, Mari," her mom orders more than suggests.

"You can, but I'm going in," and she starts to walk just as the wind picks up, catching her hair and swaying the knee-high reeds, their tussled tops waving like the waving hands of children.

"Mari, come back here," her mom demands.

But Mari continues.

She stops where she imagines the buoy line would be and turns to face her mother and sister. Her sister yells at her behind a half-opened window, "What if the water comes back? You'll drown."

Mari laughs and shouts, "No I won't." She lifts her arms and twirls, shouting, "Let the water come?"

Then, from the wide-open sky or from the wood behind the island, she hears, *You girls and your mom have held me back. I want more from life than this.* Her father's words rush over her, flooding her consciousness in an emotional tidal wave. A tidal wave she denies. Like rain hitting pavement on a hot day, it evaporates before registering.

I, she tells herself, *am not like them. Afraid of the unknown. Afraid of what comes after Dad. There has to be life after him. I have to believe that.*

"Mari, come back. You're making me nervous, and I don't like this. Your sister's right. It's dangerous. You'll be safer here with us."

The stab of familial fealty obligates Mari to assuage her mother's escalating panic. She sighs in resignation and slaloms the reeds on her exit. Having initiated an internal climate change, she now knows exactly how she'll utilize her increasingly no-longer-relevant journalism degree.

II

Fresh (Water) Start

Mari mingled in polite conversation with the members of the Great Lakes Preservation Council (GLPC) as she circled the fifth-floor room overlooking Lake Michigan and the Milwaukee Art Museum.

Milwaukee, a place Mari never expected to live, had proven acceptable, tolerable even, for the two-year residency required by her contract with the GLPC. But still, she continued to ask herself if she had accepted their offer only to escape Jake, who had already followed her to two cities in the last five years. Always, however, west of the front range. She took this job for the once-in-a-lifetime opportunity it presented, but also because she was hopeful Jake wasn't lying when he had professed, "Never. Under any circumstances will I ever live east of the Mississippi."

Lydia Ozick, the GLPC president, approached Mari, "May I have a moment of your time?"

"By all means," Mari welcomed the distraction. She followed Lydia to a quieter corner of the room with an awe-inspiring view of the museum's iconic Burke Brise Soliel's alabaster wings. "Absolutely stunning," Mari said, admiring the wings spread wide against the blue lake and a cloudless, humidity-free sky.

"Excuse me," someone said, tapping Mari on the shoulder. She gestured for the person to come in front of her as she continued *oh-ing* and *yes-ing* and *that sounds wonderful-ing* Lydia.

"Well, here he is now," Lydia said. "Rhys Jensen, I would like you to meet Mari Aehmers."

"It's nice to finally meet you, Mari," Rhys said, shaking her hand.

She returned the gesture.

"I was just telling Mari you are her personal guide for the Great Lakes region."

"Yes. It's an honor I'm delighted to assume," he said.

"As the former Lake Michigan representative for The

Great Lakes Consortium, Rhys has more knowledge of the lakes than anyone on the council," Lydia enthused. "Which, by the way, has already approved the travel itinerary he has created for you."

"Oh, how lovely. I'm looking forward to seeing it," Mari said.

"Lydia," Rhys pointed towards the podium. "I need to get Mari ready for her presentation."

"Indeed," Lydia said. "I will excuse myself."

"I've read everything you've written," Rhys shared as they crossed the room. "Quite impressive. You were a lock for the GAIA (Global Atmospheric Interdepend-ence Association) award."

It seemed surreal to Mari that something she did with the hopes of keeping her writing relevant after *Planet One* had shuttered had led her to receiving the GAIA award, along with its generous monetary gift.

"Thank you," Mari said. "I must admit, I never expected to be nominated, let alone win. I didn't think it was possible. How does writing obituaries for dying bodies of water compare to what organizations like the Arborist's Planetary Collective are documenting about climate impact on forests?"

"You're all adding so much to the narrative, but I think the love you've expressed for these lost bodies of water, along with the history you've contained in their obituaries, is a unique approach to bringing awareness to the irreversible effects of our compromised climate. Anthropomorphizing them the way you do is a brilliant touch. Personally, I think you've tapped into our universal experience of grief. You've made us aware that we need to grieve losses of nature as fervently as we grieve the loss of a loved one."

Both flattered and embarrassed by his sincere praise, she coyly asked, "I did that?" just as the toe of her shoe stuttered across the carpeting. Stumbling forward, Mari caught herself on the podium.

She recovered her composure and assumed a more professional tone. "Sometimes, I don't think it matters what any of us are documenting," she said while straightening her skirt. "If the whole thing is burning in one hemisphere and flooding in the other, who will be around to read what we've documented?"

"The environmental impacts of the last five years are mind blowing," Rhys said. "In 2023, some scientists were predicting the warming threshold of 1.5 degrees Celsius could happen as early as 2040. People didn't want to believe it. Yet here we are in 2032, a year after we crossed the threshold. Things are going to get worse." He raised a wary brow in her direction, "You can count on it."

Rhys gestured towards a chair. She sat and extracted her iPad from her bag. Rhys called the room to order, looked to Mari for a go-ahead nod, and began his introduction.

"Everyone in this room is familiar with Mari Aehmer's groundbreaking work as the final editor of the ecomagazine *Planet One*. Her unrelenting stance against the use of AI in all aspects of nature writing has led to regulations that have benefited everyone. But it is because of her personal pursuits after the closure of *Planet One* that she is here today as our newest member of the GLPC. It can be argued, and it would appear GAIA agrees, nothing she did at *Planet One* compares to what she has given us through her obituaries for the world's dying bodies of water. She has changed the lens upon which we absorb the myriad of uncomfortable truths we now face because of our shared failure to protect the only home we have. Her obituaries have united us in a shared grief."

His praise, once again, unsettled Mari to the point she stopped listening to his introduction until he said, "So, it is my honor to turn the podium over to Mari Aehmers." The room applauded as she stood.

"It is our hope," Rhys addressed her as she walked to the podium. "That you can do for the Great Lakes what you've done for the bodies of water you've written about. Only in this case, instead of writing testimonies to the deceased, we're asking you to write celebrations to the living. The GLPC has asked you here to document the life and the people of the world's largest freshwater system. Your arrival is timely. We all heard the announcement yesterday that beginning next summer, controlled migration from the southwestern U.S. to this region will begin. Members of the council, please join me in welcoming Mari Aehmers."

Mari demurred and graciously waited for their applause to end. Uncharacteristically off balance, she suddenly felt overwhelmed by the task before her. She questioned if the GLPC members' confidence in her abilities was warranted. *What if I can't write about thriving bodies of water? What if it isn't the life of water I'm drawn to?*

After a deep breath, she began by thanking the council for "what I'm sure will be a life changing experience. I had never been to the upper Midwest until moving to Milwaukee two weeks ago," she continued. "And therefore, hadn't seen any of the Great Lakes. Lake Michigan took me by surprise. It is a behemoth. I'm looking forward to visiting all the lakes and learning about the people on their shores."

After stating her credentials and her surface reasons

for accepting the position, she said, "Lydia asked me to read an excerpt from my obituary for Lake Mead, which I'm happy to do. I wrote this exclusively for GAIA's print journal *Climate Redaction*. It was published two months ago along with their announcement of my award."

"Lake Mead, one of the world's largest human-made lakes, is situated 24 miles east of Las Vegas, Nevada. Once the water source for nearly 20 million people, it became a dead pool in 2030, when its water levels fell below 895 feet. No longer able to flow over Hoover Dam, the question of the lake's bifurcation was put to rest. After two consecutive years of record-breaking heat waves in the American Southwest, Lake Mead was declared deceased in August of 2031, when its remaining puddles evaporated into the merciless atmosphere, during an otherwise anticlimactic week, with daily sustained highs of 118 degrees."

"In November of 2031, moisture-laden air over the Great Lakes region fueled an atmospheric river that stalled over Lakes Michigan and Superior for more than 24 hours. The mystics among us believed the storm contained the accumulated lost waters of Lake Mead. They say Lake Mead poured its sorrow over the land, wreaking havoc to shorelines, swallowing boats, homes, and in some cases, people. These same mystics believe that what is destroyed will destroy, and what is protected will protect. They say Lake Mead has taught us this lesson, but it's a lesson too few are willing to allow.

Lake Mead is preceded in death by his once life-sustaining cousins, the shriveled and cracked washes and creeks flowing from the Rockies to the lake. Years of limited, if any, snowmelt left them dried and impotent, unable to course water through their land-veins to their cousin.

Lake Mead is survived by his sister, Lake Mohave, who flows south from Hoover Dam to Davis Dam, and his brother Lake Havasu, who resides between Davis and Parker Dams. Sadly, his siblings are poised to flatline soon as well. Like their older, larger brother who once reigned to their north, all their relatives have been reduced to a slow drip.

Lake Mead is also survived by his father, the Green River, and his mother, the Colorado River. Like any mother, she held onto the hope that the world would acknowledge her struggling, suffering children and would decide, upon seeing her unending attempts to save them, that nothing mattered more than loving, preserving, and rescuing. But she, too, has been weakened. The people of her land continue to unapologetically tax her systems. *Why*, the mother-water wonders, *do humans choose to exploit those things that were put here with the instinctual desire to give and sustain life."*

"On a visit to Lake Mead in the summer of 2023, I chanced upon 65-year-old Nellie McBride, whom I parked next to near the long since inoperable marina at Echo Bay, a family favorite of mine from the two trips we made to Lake Mead in my childhood."

"She told me her grandfather, in need of a paycheck like so many during the 1930s, had moved his young family from Utah to Boulder City, Nevada, where he joined the construction crew of Hoover Dam. Her father, three at the time, had grown up fishing and boating on Echo Bay. Proud of their association with Hoover Dam, her family had remained either in Boulder City or Las Vegas. Now a resident of Grand Junction, Colorado, she left Boulder City in 2021, when 'to anyone paying attention,' she claimed, "it was obvious Lake Mead would be a dead pool before the end of the decade. We had to leave," she added. Her gaze long across the barren scape. "Before there was no more electricity. No more water. I hope all the hay was worth it."

"In the year Nellie McBride left Boulder City, the Colorado River was drained of more than two trillion gallons of water used to irrigate alfalfa fields, covering nearly three million acres of crops in the Colorado River Basin states."

"Nellie's parting words to me, speak to a collective grief around the loss of such a well-loved lake. 'Like so many species, plants, and waterbeds before it,' she said, her feet disrupting dust on the parched ground, "humanity drove Lake Mead to its end. Why is it only now, as it's dying, does it seem like people recognize its loss and wonder what more could've been done to save it?"

At that moment, *something* happened to Mari. Some kind of weird word association took her from the luncheon and placed her in Old Lady Carlson's yard. The spinster neighbor of her childhood. *Why am I here?* Mari wondered, as the words dried, cracked, and parched echoed in her ears.

Mari, now seven, is standing in front of Old Lady Carlson, whose mouth is moving but makes no sound. She looks down at Old Lady Carlson's feet, which don red flip flops.

Young Mari scrutinizes the deep crevices of dried, cracked skin that surround the bottoms of the old woman's feet. Mari looks at Old Lady Carlson's skin-cracking, swollen fingers, her blotched arms, her wrinkled and puckered face, her wiry, gray hair. Everything about Old Lady Carlson is dehydrated.

The lever on Mari's memory view-finder switches and she is sitting in her therapist's office five years ago.

"My mother has this way of assuming everyone experiences things the same way she does," Mari says. "In her mind, I'm

experiencing the divorce like she is. Like I've been left by my husband,
instead of having been rejected by my father."

"As a result," her therapist says, "you've been disabled. Your
mother's feelings have usurped your own. You are not conscious of
your feelings; and therefore, you have no idea how they motivate your
behaviors."

The lever is pushed again. She's standing in the drained bed of
Lake Wapello. Mari's mother is demanding that she returns to the
beach. She doesn't want to do her mother's bidding, but feels obligated
to mitigate the woman's intensifying panic. Mari sighs in resignation
and walks out of the empty lakebed. She looks down to find her feet
are dried and cracked like Old Lady Carlson's, but different. Her
feet and legs are transforming into the dried bed of Lake Wapello.
All moisture is extracted from her body. She dissolves into a million
grains of sand before reaching her mother.

"And so," she found herself mentally present at the
luncheon again, "I'm excited to do this work for you and
I'm sure I'll come to love these remarkable lakes." She
turned her body towards the window overlooking Lake
Michigan and said, "As you...all...." Before she could
finish her sentence, her throat closed, stifling a scream.
Gripped in terror by the sight of a tidal wave about to
engulf the building, Mari fainted.

Moments later, Mari opened her eyes to find Lydia
pressing a cold cloth to her forehead and Rhys holding her
hand. "A medic is on the way," he said.

"Oh, I don't need a medic. At least, I don't think so.
What happened?"

"One minute you were saying how excited you are to
be here and the next, you were on the floor," Rhys told
her.

As her head cleared, Mari remembered her out-of-
body experience, followed by the illusion of the wave. She

thought it best not to tell her new employers the truth. Instead, she opted to say, "Perhaps I was hungrier than I thought. I can be hypoglycemic at times."

III

Four Months Later

1

Scheduled to leave for the Door County peninsula that afternoon, Mari was packing when her phone rang.

"Hey, Sara. I'm glad it's you. Jake's been texting and calling the past several days. It's kind of creeping me out." She zipped her bag and asked, "What's up?"

"Mom's behind on her taxes again," Sara cut to the chase.

"Big surprise there," Mari said. "You know, if Mom can't afford her house, she needs to sell it and get a place she can. Actually Sara," Mari, barely concealing her agitation over this never-ending situation, added, "I'm pretty certain she can afford her house, and she's just playing you."

"Not this again?"

"Look, she never ever asks me for money. She never tells me about any of her money problems because, and I know you're going to hate this when I say it, but she plays me differently."

"You know, your therapy really messed you up. What the hell do you mean, she plays you differently?"

"In my conversations with her, she's always doing just fine financially. She doesn't need anything. And it's not until after you pay for something, like her taxes, that I hear about it. Then, she has some off-the-wall story of persecution that caused her to be late or unable to pay. She always claims that she didn't ask you to help her out. She claims you did it because you love her, and because you enjoy being able to help her."

"Of course, she gets you to pay for things through dubious, passive-aggressive means," Mari said. "But my larger point is, I know she's asking you for the money, but she wants me to believe you're doing it of your own volition. To me, she presents herself as a financially sound victim. To you, she's an un-financially-sound victim. Why do you think that is? Whenever I stick up for you, and I ask her why she's taking your money, since, according to my conversations with her, she doesn't need it, she gets agitated and evasive, and blames Dad for everything."

"What are you driving at?"

"Press Mom on whether or not she really needs the money, and I think you'll find out," Mari took a deep breath.

In a more measured tone, she continued, "Sara, I think Mom's holding onto the house because she believes that's how she'll keep us from abandoning her. She's always saying as long as she has the house, we'll always have a place to go. Doesn't that strike you as odd? You own your home, and I've lived on my own for a decade. She's just waiting for you to divorce David and move back in with her, or for my work to dry up, which she believes would force me to move in with her. I will never let our mother starve, but she's only 60. If she wants to stay in that house, it's her job, not yours or mine, to figure out a way to do it."

Her phone pinged. It was Jake. "Mari, please stop ghosting me," he texted. "I'm just curious about your new job. I hope Milwaukee suits you. I still really care about you."

Why, she wanted to scream, *won't you leave me alone?*

In a fit, she paced. Scratching her now hive-spotted neck, she said, "Mom has decided to extract everything from us she can, both financially and emotionally. When Dad left her, she married you, and you became her enabler, but I'm not going to. I'm not her spouse. I'm not her therapist. I'm not her confessor. And I'm not her peer. I'm her daughter! And I wish, just once in my life, she would act like my goddamn parent!"

"Are you finished?" The sarcasm in Sara's voice echoed throughout Mari's apartment.

"Yes."

"You know, I don't think we have much to complain about. We never wanted for anything as far as food, clothing, and shelter were concerned."

Mari's brain exploded, "That's the low-hanging fruit!"

"And Dad *is* an asshole who has screwed half the women in this town. Mom never cheated on him. He was mean to her, and to all of us, and she's not been able to get over it."

Mari, her voice raw, said, "And it's not our job to soak it up for her. She needs to go to a therapist and figure out why she *won't* let it go. It's hard, impossible in fact, to work with someone who almost daily states, 'I will never get over what your father did to us,' and 'I'm never leaving this house.' She wants to stay stuck in that moment. I don't. And, whether or not either of you thinks so, it's not healthy for any of us that she does."

And now, Sara held nothing back.

"I'm so sick and tired of listening to you. Ever since you've had therapy you act like a goddamn know-it-all. Like you know what everyone else needs. What Mom needs is for you to understand what she's been through and just do what she wants. Can't you just do that? You complain, but you're not even here. You know what I wish? I wish I could get away from here, for just a weekend. But every time I decide to do something, Mom has something she needs me to do. I swear to God, all I have to do is think I might do something and she's texting me about this or that, and shit…I just give up after awhile. At least you can use your job as an excuse. So, what I need from you, is for you to be *my* goddamn sister and do *your* fucking part with our mother, so I can have a break!" and with that, Sara disconnected the call.

Exasperated, Mari texted Lydia she'd be late and to expect her closer to lunch. As she sent it, another text from Jake arrived. It read, "Text or call, Mari. I really need to talk. Jake."

It was his third text that morning. He exuded the same needy pull as her mother, and it infuriated her.

"Why won't you leave me alone? I ended it. For good. I wasn't joking," she yelled at her phone. And then, remembering the look on his face when she said no to his proposal, a look that wasn't sad or disappointed but defiant, unwilling to accept her answer, she opened her settings, scrolled to block contacts, and entered his name.

Mari splayed on the floor, closed her eyes, and welcomed the warmth from the shaft of light she had landed beneath. She longed for the dry, barren landscapes of the dying waters she had been drawn to. They felt safe to her. She liked that all was exposed. There were no secrets, other than by the industries and governments who chose profits over the environment. They had secrets and plenty of them. At least the death of the global waters exposed their lies and prevarications. She wondered what it would take to expose her father's secrets. He had many. She knew she had half-siblings. In fact, she was more than certain she'd dated one in high school.

Her mother had secrets too. Less malevolent secrets, but equally destructive. She lied and manipulated, and conflated and inflated truths, all to protect her hidden agendas.

Without effort, her surroundings faded, and she found herself floating in the Dead Sea, long since extinct as a viable body of water.

The coarseness of the water supports her weight. Its salinity stings her back. She stands and walks across the sea's parched expanse. Beautiful salt sculptures dot the scape. Salt mushrooms, she calls them.

Mari gazes over the withered terrain towards Jordan and decides she is tired of feeling the darkness that surrounds her family. She wants to believe that everything is revealed if she keeps herself dry and barren like the dead lakebeds. She wants to believe that places everything on the surface. But Mari does not account for the necessity of flow; and she, with great aptitude, discounts what she is terrified of.

"But you've barely begun to understand your feelings, let alone feel them," her therapist, suddenly standing next to her, says. "You're confused as to where your feelings have taken refuge. You can't rationalize away your feelings," her therapist continues. "One way or another they will overwhelm the barrier you've constructed between you and them."

Her therapist dissipates as a man appears, walking towards her.

She shields her eyes from the sun in hopes of discerning who he is.

"Jake?" Mari calls out. "Is that you? Why are you here? I'm done with you. I'm done with us."

He doesn't answer, but stops about fifty yards away. His arms to his sides.

Perplexed by his unflinching stance, Mari scrambles her mind to understand why the two of them are standing in the dead Dead Sea.

"I'm sorry, but I want you to leave me alone. For good. No more calls. No more texts. We're over." She raises her arms and says, "For the love of God, please respect my wishes."

The thrumming is low and quiet at first. The rumble of the ground, faint. Before she comprehends the nature of her situation, waves crash over them from opposite directions. With speed and force, the water carries them away from one another.

Sweating and shaking, she returned to the present moment.

2

"I'm certain you'll love Door County," Lydia said, handing Mari her itinerary.

"Every place I've visited so far has been beautiful, so my expectations are high," she smiled at Lydia. Glancing at the itinerary, and in a conscious attempt to distract Lydia from inquiring about her trip to the Upper Peninsula and Lake Superior, she said, "I see Rhys is joining me in a few days."

Mari remembered little of Lake Superior other than her initial vision of its cobalt blue expanse. As soon as she had stepped off the bridge that crossed the Two Hearted River and crested a small dune, the lake swelled into a massive wave and Mari, overcome with vertigo, retraced her tracks as fast as her spinning head had allowed.

"Yes. His aunt lives in Ephraim. He knows the Door County Peninsula well. He said he's looking forward to taking you to Washington Island. Do be sure to visit the Fragrant Isle Lavendar Farm. Trust me, you won't want to leave it. It's so pleasant sitting among all the lavender. The scent, as you can imagine, is wonderful, but it's the buzzing of all the bees that heightens the experience. It's a lulling, soporific place."

Two years of paid travel to tour the Great Lakes and learn about the people who loved them, while positing, along with Rhys, her recently assigned coauthor, the possible effects of what was sure to be a massive migration from coastal cities and the southwest to the world's largest fresh water supply was inarguably a sweet gig. She liked Rhys as a co-worker, but lately being around him made her uncomfortable. Rhys and water caused her stomach fluids to undulate to the point of nausea. In the presence of both, her self-control began to unravel. She didn't have to control others but the idea of losing control of herself frightened her. Rhys was starting to frighten her. The water was frightening her. Her increasing visions and out-of-body experiences were frightening her. To say she was out of sorts was an understatement, which left her wishing Rhys wasn't joining her.

"You have three weeks in Ephraim," Lydia said. "I was going to have you stay at a lodge in Baileys Harbor, but it fell victim to the atmospheric river a few years ago."

"I visited a location in Racine yesterday. The beach erosion from that storm caused condos to plunge into Lake

Michigan. I was told five people died," Mari said.

"That's true. That was a big news story when it happened. Obviously. But it wasn't a singular story. It happened up and down both sides of the coast. Luckily, we haven't had a repeat of that storm since, but it's only a matter of time," Lydia said, as she stood up. "I've booked you at the Eagle Harbor Inn in Ephraim. Early August is a busy time for the whole peninsula, so I couldn't get you a waterfront room. It's a lovely place. I've stayed there myself. It's tucked in the woods just off highway 42. The bay is right across the street."

"Oh, I'm certain it will be lovely," Mari enthused. "I love the woods."

She found the drive to Ephraim peaceful and easy. But the calm rustled something inside her. An inarticulate message knocked against the back of her consciousness like a wave ebbing and flowing. She fought the water metaphors. She was sick of them. They were everywhere around her lately. Since she was staying in the woods, she told herself it was more like a tree being shaken from its base. The message wasn't clear, until it was. And she didn't like what she heard, so she stomped it back down into the dirt.

It said this: *Your therapist was right. You left therapy too soon.*

IV

The Source

1

Mari, tucked away in her wood-ensconced suite, had barely ventured out since arriving in Ephraim three days ago. Everything and everyone haunted her. She felt the needy pulls from her mother. Her sister. Jake. She felt hostility from her father. Somehow, in his abandonment of her, she had let him down. She wasn't, as he had said, "The daughter I had hoped for. As a matter of fact, Stacy (his new wife's adult daughter) is ten times the daughter you've ever been." *What exactly does that even mean?* she wondered.

The bay was, unfortunately, right across the street. Unusually high winds rushed foam-crested waves to the shore where they broke and spilled onto the beach, then fanned and thinned, stretching inland until the ravenous bay drew them back. All of it, the motion, the roar of the waves, the slapping against the sand, the giving and the taking, swirled in her head and stomach.

The National Weather Service's rip tide alert was reason enough for Mari to lounge around her suite, reading books and watching episodes of the various iterations of *Star Trek,* until three o'clock on Thursday when Rhys knocked on her door.

Eager and smiling, he asked "Do you like root beer floats?"

"Hello to you too," she said.

He repeated the question.

"Yes, I suppose. I haven't had one in years."

"Great. Are you up for a walk and a float?"

"Sure," she laughed.

As they walked, Mari asked him about the various stores and landmarks to their right to avoid looking at the bay to their left.

"That's where we're going," Rhys pointed up ahead. "To Wilson's. They have the best root beer floats on the peninsula," he said.

By the time they arrived at the restaurant patio, all thoughts of high winds, rip tides, Jake, and her family had dissolved.

"This place is really cute," she said, after they ordered.

Red and white stripes and gingham dominated the décor. The building appeared to be a lake cottage that had been converted and expanded.

"It hasn't changed in my lifetime," Rhys said. "Not the tablecloths nor the food. It's all happiness for me here. Ephraim in general, not just Wilson's."

The waitress placed two frosted mugs on the table.

"This does look good," Mari said. "Okay," she admitted after a couple of bites. "This is the best root beer float I've ever had."

"It's all in the simple pleasures," Rhys smiled at her. "Has the wind been this bad the whole time you've been here?"

"Yeah," she sighed. Rhys had undone her mood with two sentences.

The fact that her parents had ruined all the childhood places where she had found happiness and had destroyed her ability to find joy in simple pleasures had not fully registered with her until hearing, and seeing, someone say those things with unquestionable sincerity.

Sadness overtook her. She pushed her mug away.

"Whoa. What just happened to you? Are you okay?"

Damn his earnestness, Mari thought.

A hundred things to say rushed through her mind. She settled on, "I don't like this job, Rhys."

Stunned, he straightened and asked, "Why?"

Don't abandon yourself by hiding behind half-truths and sleights of phrase, her therapist wormed her way in and reminded her.

Mari, tired of the intrusion, mentally fought back, *I've been out of therapy for two years, I've ended my relationship with Jake, and was doing quite well, thank you, until now. Until the water. Until Rhys.*

She sensed her therapist across from her, brows raised, and waiting.

Okay, Mari thought, *we'll play it your way.*

"Remember when I fainted?" she asked Rhys.

"Of course."

"I wasn't hungry. I experienced this weird astral projection of sorts while giving my speech. I fainted because I saw a huge wave about to crash through the windows. Obviously, it wasn't real, but ever since I've been here, I've been having all these strange visions of drowning and of being at this lake where my family went when I was a kid. Recently, my ex showed up in one. I just feel like, if I could get away from the water, it would all go away and I'd be fine."

She went on to explain her childhood visits to Lake

Wapello and her recent visions, and how her mother and sister were afraid the water would return and drown her. "The visions ring true. They always want me nearby in real life. They're always projecting their fears onto me. But the truth is, I was never afraid of the water as a kid, and now I am. Just the idea of looking at the bay makes me nervous."

"My vision with Jake, my ex, was different though," she continued. "We were at the Dead Sea. He's just standing there while I'm shouting at him that I'm done with our relationship. Then, these two enormous waves engulf us from different directions and carry us away."

"Was your breakup acrimonious?"

Mari sighed, "Yes and no. He refuses to accept that I don't want to marry him. He blames it on the fact that my father abandoned me, causing me to have attachment issues. He's not wrong about the attachment issues, but he's passive-aggressive and manipulative like my mother, and verbally abusive like my father. So I wouldn't attach to him regardless."

"C'mon," he said, standing up.

"Where are we going?"

"You need to meet my aunt. She lives about a quarter of a mile north on 42."

"Why do I need to meet your aunt?"

"She's a bit of a mystic herself."

"So, you think I'm a mystic?" she asked, following him out of Wilson's.

"Don't you?" He smiled and stopped at the crosswalk. "It isn't so bad today, but wait until Friday. It will be a constant stream of cars from Sister Bay to Egg Harbor. "Let's go," he said, once traffic in both directions had paused.

They followed the walk along the bay in silence until

they turned east and ascended a steep hill.

"It's amazing how quiet it becomes once you're away from the bay," Mari said.

Rhys nodded.

"Does your aunt live here alone?"

"Sort of. I'm here more than I'm in Milwaukee. I stay in her guest house. The property has been in my family for years. My grandparents purchased it in the early 1950s, and left it to my dad and his sister, my Aunt Clara. My dad doesn't want the property, so he signed his half over to me. I'm an only child, and Clara," he paused, "no longer has children. So, the property will be mine, eventually."

"Your aunt no longer has children?"

"That's her story to tell, but yes, she no longer has children."

They passed two drives with ever increasing vertical drops to the bay. "Next drive is Aunt Clara's," Rhys said, gesturing to the right.

"It's beautiful here. And the aroma," she inhaled the scent of pine and ash and birch and water and earth, "is divine."

As they descended the drive, Mari welcomed the intermittent cool caused by an overhead canopy of trees, casting a latticework of light and dark angles across the length and width of the drive. She thought the environment seemed a perfect home for fairy folk.

"So, do you think you'll ever get married?" Mari surprised herself. "Sorry, that was a little personal."

"No worries. I do want to get married again, someday."

"Again?"

"I was married for a year. Been divorced for two."

"What happened?"

"Let's just say she didn't believe me when I said this is where I want to spend most of my weekends and all of my retirement, and I believed her when she said she loved it here."

Rhys stopped at the bottom of the hill, "I love this view of the bay."

Mari hazarded a look. Its tide, calmer in the wanning afternoon, didn't seem as threatening.

"I was rather naïve, I suppose," he said.

With a quizzical slant of her head, Mari stared at Rhys's sunlit profile. "What do you mean?"

"I've spent all my life around trustworthy people," he said, and turned to face her. "I had no reason for doubting her sincerity."

"Funny," Mari chuckled. "I've spent my whole life around untrustworthy people. I'm working hard to dispel the assumption that everyone will lie before they'll tell the truth. Dysfunctional, I know. But hey, that's one of the maligned truths my parents passed on to me."

"I wish you luck with that," his eyes met hers when he said it.

She searched for an ironic tone in his words or a flippancy in his manners but found none.

"C'mon. You're gonna love my aunt," he turned to round the trees.

Impulsively, she grabbed his arm, "Wait."

He turned back. "What is it?"

A roiling started low in her belly as fear inched northward through her torso. Her mind, respecting her anxiety, instructed her to say, *Oh, it's nothing. Never mind.* But her mouth betrayed her, and asked, "Can I tell you something?"

"Absolutely," his concerned response heightened her

anxiety.

"I've never told anyone this," she laced and unlaced her fingers. If she had a tissue, she'd shred it. "I guess because it seemed like it was a game on his part. A passive-aggressive attempt to get me to take the ring. Or to stay in Boulder, at least. But he scared me. Game or not, it really creeped me out."

For a moment, she was sitting in her therapist's office the day of her final visit.

"We can't own something. Truly own it. Until we speak it," her therapist said.

"I know that's true. But haven't I owned enough?" Mari asked.

"If you're really asking, I have to say, no. You're leaving therapy too soon," her therapist emphasized the words *too soon.* *"You've convinced yourself that you've stopped intellectualizing everything. I'm here to tell you that's not true. Some things yes, but only the things you're comfortable with feeling."*

"Mari," Rhys's voice interrupted her recollection. "I'm sorry, but I don't understand. What, exactly, scared you?"

Tell him, her therapist wormed her way into the present moment. *You can trust him.*

Mari's therapist had never lied to her. She might have said things Mari didn't like or want to hear, but she had never lied to her.

Okay, she thought. *What have I got to lose?*

Nothing and everything! her therapist joyfully exclaimed.

You can go away, now, Lynn, Mari ordered. But somewhere inside her, she understood the paradox her therapist alluded to.

"I'd told him countless times I didn't want to marry him," she began. Tiny blotches appeared on her shorts where she had been rubbing her sweaty palms. She felt hives heating her neck.

This is where Lynn would tell me to stay focused, breathe, and keep going, Mari told herself. Despite the mounting nausea she felt, she inhaled, forced the air down through her feet, and willed herself to keep going.

"He knew before he proposed to me that I'd say no, and so, before I answered, he told me that if I said no, he didn't want to live; and, he didn't want me to live either because it pained him to think of me having a life without him in it. Weird right? Not him having a life without me in it. Then, he told me he was done with this world anyway and suggested we could leave it together. He proposed a double suicide to me."

She lowered her eyes, "I'd been hedging my response to the GLPC anyway, but the next day, I accepted the position and left Boulder as soon as I could."

Dumbfounded, Rhys turned back to the bay.

It was in his silence that her subconscious began to scratch against her conscious mind. Shame, an emotion she had chosen for years not to acknowledge, forced its way out of darkness far enough that it flushed her cheeks and overwhelmed her with regret.

"I'm sorry," she said, and filled the void with babbling. "I shouldn't have said anything. I mean, it's so crazy and out there. Right? Who knows? I'm sure I'm making..."

"Whoa. Slow down," Rhys said, putting his hands on her shoulders. "It is that crazy. It's also controlling, possessive, and demented if you ask me."

Rhys continued to talk. Mari ceased to listen. Rhys's words were drowned out by the loud shaming voice yelling inside her head. *That's a fine way to make Rhys think you're nuts. He's lost all respect for you now. You know he's asking himself what kind of person would get involved with someone like Jake? You've ruined any kind of friendship that was building between you. He's probably, right now, at this minute, hoping you will resign.*

Her self-berating attack ended when she heard him say, "C'mon. Now, I know you have to meet my aunt."

Clara's house came into full view as they rounded the line of trees. Nestled between the bay and the hill, its arts and crafts styled architecture with its large front porch beckoned visitors to take refuge. Mari thought the guest cabin, situated to the left of the house and similar in style, appeared quite cozy and warm. But the yard! The yard caused Mari's jaw to drop.

Dozens of clay and cement statues, scattered across the front and side lawns, faced the bay. Some with searching eyes. Some with content eyes. Some with sad eyes. Mothers holding children. Husbands and wives embraced. Husband and wives in various stages of departure. Children running. Children playing marbles. Children dismembered, like puzzle pieces on the ground that needed fitting back together. Fishing boats up-righted. Fishing boats capsized. Through it all, expressions of lament and joy were perfectly balanced. Adding to the figures' allure were the vibrant colors of broken tiles, pieces of China, stones, gems, and sea glass used to enhance the statues' facial features and clothes. These colors fueled the anger, delight, suffering, playfulness, remorse, and contentment that emanated from the more than a hundred statues populating the yard; their laughter and wailing, audible to a keen ear tuned to their frequency.

"I gather your aunt is an artist," she said, zigzagging through the statues.

"She calls herself a folk artist, but yes," Rhys beamed with pride.

Mari paused in front of a six-posted cement fence. Each post was topped with a woman's head tilted back.

Three had their eyes squeezed tight in agony; their mouths, open ovals howling in distress. The other three had their eyes and mouths closed; their peaceful countenances delighting in the warmth of the sun.

"Aunt Clara says the fence represents women before and after acceptance of their truth," Rhys said, as he stepped onto the porch and opened the screen door. "Aunt Clara," he sang her name. "I've brought a guest."

"Excellent. I'm preparing tea and cookies now," his aunt called from the kitchen.

Mari stepped into the foyer. Everything about the house, from the sunken living room to the dining room table set into an expansive bay window, from the built-in shelving full of books to the oak-mantled fireplace topped with a flower-filled vase, from the smell of cinnamon, molasses and ginger permeating the house to the cool colors surrounding her, it all infused Mari with a sense of peace and comfort.

"Your aunt's an artist, to be sure," Mari said. "But clearly, she's also a master of hygge."

Clara came from the kitchen with a large tray and set it on the table.

After Rhys introduced the two, Mari, drawn to the aquamarine pendant Clara wore, said "That's a lovely necklace. The gem is a perfect sphere. It's mesmerizing."

"Thank you," Clara said, lifting it from her chest. She cupped it in her palm. "It has served me well."

"Served you well?" Mari questioned.

"Aquamarine brings a person courage and prepares them to receive love and joy and peace. My peace has been restored."

Mari nodded in understanding. She used to have an amethyst with her all the time to help relieve her stress. She couldn't recollect when, exactly, she had stopped carrying it.

The trio shared a pleasant conversation over tea and warm molasses cookies. For what felt like the first time in her life outside of therapy, Mari was experiencing an irony free conversation, absent of any mockery or sarcastic jabs.

"The recipe dates back three generations," Clara said, after Mari had commented on how delicious the cookies were.

Mari searched her memory for something as comforting as these cookies three generations old on either side of her family. Upon recalling that her maternal grandmother had been a fabulous cook, baker, and gardener, she heard her mother's repeated excuse for always serving Ragu and TV dinners echoing in her ears, *I was never very interested in cooking or gardening.*

Unfortunately, her grandmother died before Mari was old enough to know how much she would long for her homemade egg noodles and gravy piled over a heap of mashed potatoes. And her pies! No one made a crust like her grandmother and, since her mother took no interest, she didn't even have the recipe to pass on.

"I need to get something out of the guest house," Rhys said. He stood and pushed his chair into the table. "Mari, I'm sure my aunt would welcome hearing about your visions."

"I'd love to hear about them," Clara said, clapping her hands together.

"Well, um…" Mari hesitated at length, but Clara's unchanged demeanor, her nonjudgemental, Buddhaesque calm, and the surroundings buoyed Mari, and she shared everything. Her familial history. Her relationship with Jake. Her therapy. Her reasons for accepting GLPC's offer. Her visions and astral projections. Her desire to resign.

"Do all of your visions center around water?" Clara asked.

"Yes," Mari said. "I don't know what it is about water and me."

"Really?" Clara asked. Her tone suggested Mari should know.

"Really. I don't," Mari said.

"When you were at Lake Wapello as a child, were you a water girl or a beach girl?" Clara asked.

"Water all the way," Mari said.

"Did you ever pretend to be a fish or a shark or anything?"

Mari had to coax the memory into her consciousness. "Yes," she finally said. Her body relaxed, and her physiognomy transformed as youthful joy filled her entire being. Smiling, and far away, she said, "Somedays I was a dolphin, breaching and spinning with my pod. Other days I was a narwhal, exploring hidden worlds in the Artic with my blessing." She wiped away a solitary tear, and breathed more than said, "I haven't thought about that in years."

Clara looked out over the bay, yellowing in the late afternoon sun. "I once turned away from my water magic too," she said. "When my husband and son drowned in the bay, I didn't want to feel the pain. My loss was so immense. And I blamed myself for mistaking their flailing arms as waving. They were too far out for me to distinguish until it was too late. So I shut the spigot and stopped my flow. I denied myself water's incredible power to heal. I forgot the emotional awakening and the spiritual purification water brings to not just the body, but the mind and soul as well. I closed all the bay facing curtains and never looked at the water. I lost my way. I almost sold the property," Clara stopped and warmed their tea.

Mari sat quietly, reverently, amazed by Clara's ability and her willingness to share her experience. Her mom and sister never wanted to talk about anything other than what her father had done to them, condemning them all to live in the perpetual aftermath of her father's abandonment. Her mother still used the divorce as the default excuse for the adverse situations she created.

"Well, if your father hadn't left me," she would say. "We wouldn't be in this mess." Mari found her mother's use of pronouns endlessly interesting.

Anytime Mari suggested her mother and sister needed counseling, her mother would say, "No one can understand what we've been through."

"Right," Mari would retort. "Because you're the only person who's ever been left by her husband."

At this, brainwashed Sara would rush to her mother's defense, "Our case is unique. Mom's right. People just don't understand."

Clara sipped her tea. "We all need water to live, obviously," she said. "We, and the planet, after all, are mostly water. But some of us, like you and me, are ruled by the element of water. You're afraid the water is going to crash through that dam you've constructed to protect your heart from your wounding, but in order to restore your body's motion, in order to live again, you must feel the pain your parents have caused you. You must allow that pain to wash over you and pass through you. Otherwise, you're as emotionally dehydrated as all the dead seas and lakes you write about. I get the sense you've denied your true spirit, which is at home in deep waters where your emotional currents freely flow. You have water magic, too, you know. That means you have the power to call the water to you.

But your visions suggest you have forsaken that magic and have retreated to the shallows for the sake of your mom and sister."

Unable to deny the veracity of Clara's words, sorrow and truth converged, fissuring Mari's dam into a myriad of pieces. Pieces of anger, resentment, shame, guilt, longing, grief, and isolation.

"Come with me to the sofa, Mari," Clara said.

She stood and followed Clara. Mari's trembling body was unsteady from the once dormant currents now pulsating throughout her. On the sofa, Clara wrapped Mari in a blanket. Unable to calm her hands, the throw's fringe quivered as Mari pulled it to her chin.

Clara embraced Mari. "I'm here to tell you, you will not drown."

And with that, her dam fully ruptured, putting the question of Mari's bifurcation to rest.

2

Red-eyed, she thanked Rhys for the ride back to Eagle Harbor Inn.

"I wasn't expecting all that when I agreed to meet your aunt," she grinned, and stepped away from his car.

"Oh, I almost forgot," Rhys said, reaching into his pocket. "Here," he handed her Clara's necklace. "She said the two of you were ready for each other."

Mari clasped it in her palm. "I consider this quite a gift," she said. "Please, give her my thanks."

"Will do. And, just for the record, I hope you decide to stay."

Mari looked through the trees towards the bay.

"If I do," she said, turning back to him, "will you take

me to the lavender farm?"

"Absolutely," he said.

She waved goodbye as he drove towards a burst of purple-fringed clouds set above the gloaming orange-yellow-pink horizon.

Exhausted, Mari went straight to bed and effortlessly succumbed to sleep.

In that liminal space between sleeping and waking, when the subconscious recedes and the conscious mind rises, Mari found herself, once again, walking into the dried bed of Lake Wapello.

"I wish they wouldn't have drained the lake," she calls to her mom, standing on the beach. "It's a perfect day for swimming."

"Mari, come back. Your sister is right. This could be dangerous. You're scaring us."

"I'm not scared," Mari says.

"Well, I am," her mom snaps.

"This is too creepy for me," Sara shouts from the car. "Come back so we can get out of here."

The stab of familial fealty obligates Mari to want to assuage her mother's escalating panic. She reluctantly complies. As she walks towards her mother, Mari feels her toes splay into the sand. She looks down to find her feet transformed, three toes pointed forward and one pointed back. She stops.

A harsh, raspy, "Skeow! Skeow! Skeow!" explodes from the beach.

Bewildered, Mari looks up to find her mom and sister gone. Two herons, beating their wings and stomping their feet, appear to be yelling at her.

Frightened, Mari backs up. As she does, she feels her five toes once again pressing into the sand. She hears her mom and sister begging her to return to the shore.

Then, from the wide-open sky or the wood behind the island, she hears Clara say, "You are not a heron. Call forth the waters and return home."

She watches her mother pace and fret, while her sister's eyes, from above the half-open window, implore Mari not to leave her.

Join me, she wants to call out, but drops to her knees instead, overcome with the reality that their fears will never allow it. Herons never leave the shallows. They prefer isolation. Mari will visit the shallows from time to time, but her nature necessitates depth and rotation and tide and the company of many.

"Mom. Sara. I love you, but I can't be the person you want me to be," she calls out through tears. "I know you'll think I'm abandoning you, but I'm not. If I stay here, if I do what you want me to do, I will be abandoning myself. I have been abandoning myself. I can't do it any longer."

"We don't understand you, Mari," her mom shouts. "Come back here now."

Mari stands and turns her back to them. With the mere lift of her arms, she beckons the water forth. Waves circle round the island and come at her from both sides. This time, she doesn't faint. This time, she closes her eyes and welcomes the rush of water over her.

Flow

There was a woman reborn to water, who remembered how to ebb and flow with ease and grace and how to not question the moon's push and pull of her emotional tides. On some days she inhabited her dolphin spirit and swam fast and free, her fins cutting the water as her flukes propelled her into a full body breach. Her rostrum high, inhaling the sun-heated air. With gleeful whistles, she arced wide and spun before returning to the surface. She was one of many in her pod. On other days, she evoked her narwhal spirit and remembered she was magical, a unicorn of the sea. On these days, she slowed and found pleasure exploring the depths of Artic waters with the other mystical, elusive creatures in her blessing.

Acknowledgements

Writing requires space and time, and I cannot thank Write On, Door County enough for my residency, which afforded me both. This book exists, in part, due to my time at Write On.

Many thanks to Ariana Den Bleyker and ELJ Editions for giving *Born of Water* a home, and to Diane Gottlieb for all she has done to support this project.

Much love to my writing group, Al Kratz, Audra Kerr Brown, Karen Jones, Lisa Alletson, and Dan Crawley. My appreciation for your friendship and insightful feedback is immeasurable. Special thanks to Al and Audra (We are the corn-fed, Iowa-bred trio.) for being my go-to emergency readers. I would also like to thank my dear friends Amy Daniels and Melissa Ostrom for their thoughtful, caring feedback on Part One.

Thanks to Kim Suhr and the Red Oak Writing community.

Many hugs and kisses to my daughter Hannah for her illustrations.

Lastly, I am forever grateful to my husband for climbing the cliff with me. Every day with our daughter proves the climb was worth it.

About the Author

Constance Malloy is the creator of The Burning Hearth Blog and the editor of *Voices of the Summer Solstice*. Her flash can be found at *Emerge Literary Journal, New Flash Fiction Review,* and *Bending Genres.* She can be found by the river, in the woods, or by the lake. She can also be found at constancemalloy.com and on X @ConstanceMall13.

Made in the USA
Monee, IL
23 June 2024

59876193R00049